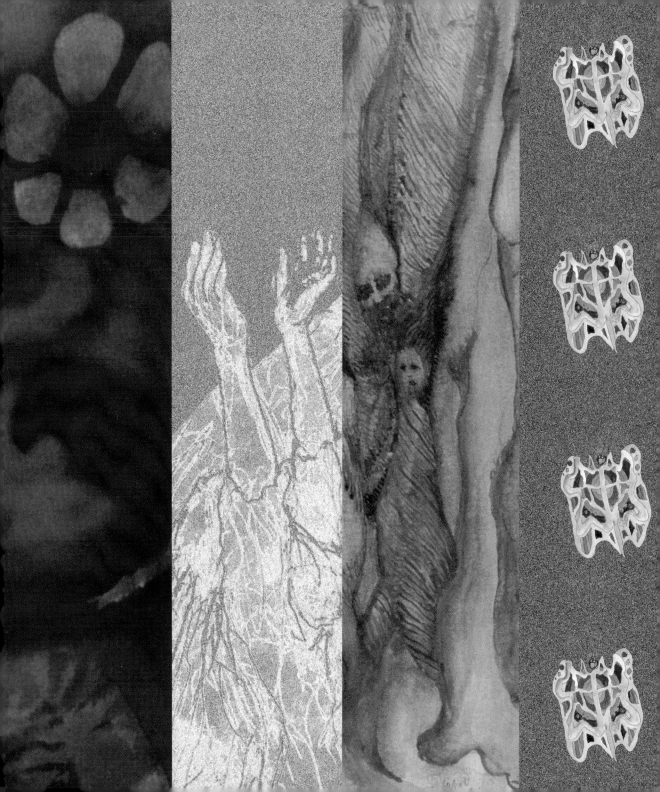

JERRY GARCIA'S

Amazing Grace

lyrics by
John Newton

song arranged and
performed by
**Jerry Garcia,
David Grisman,**
and
Tony Rice

artwork by
Jerry Garcia

HarperCollinsPublishers

May we

walk in

grace and

beauty

Jerry Garcia's Amazing Grace
Introduction copyright © 2002 by
the Estate of Jerome J. Garcia.
Compilation copyright © 2002 by
the Estate of Jerome J. Garcia.
Illustrations copyright © 2002 by
the Estate of Jerome J. Garcia.
Printed in China. All rights reserved.
www.harpercollins.com

Library of Congress
Cataloging-in-Publication Data
Garcia, Jerry (date).   [Amazing
grace]   Jerry Garcia's amazing grace.
p.   cm.   An illustrated version of
the hymn written by John Newton.
ISBN 0-06-029710-7   1. Hymns,
English—Texts.   2. Grace (Theology)
—Poetry.   3. Christian poetry,
English.   [1. Hymns.]   I. Newton,
John, 1725–1807. Amazing grace.
II. Title.   BV317.A49 G37 2001
2001016641   264'.23–dc21

Typography by Carla Weise
1 2 3 4 5 6 7 8 9 10
❖
First Edition

Introduction

The elements of loss and redemption run through Jerry Garcia's life more intensely than most people's—his sad childhood when his father drowned, and he was stricken with asthma, his hard-earned success with its bitter, lonely fruit, and the joy he created during his decades of playing music.

What is grace? It's a part of our lives. A graceful woman, a gracious host, a grace note, a grace period, all somehow create a sense of space, of potential, of goodness. Jerry and I were both raised Catholic during the 40s and 50s, "Hail Mary, full of grace" times, when the Church retained its mystical teeth. We learned very young about the ins and outs of the State of Grace. Grace was what you needed to get to heaven.

When Jerry and I were first getting to know each other in the mid-1970s, we compared Catholic childhoods. "Did you have the milk bottle?" I asked him.

"The milk bottle! Yes, we had that," he replied, and we laughed as we remembered the lesson on grace, the nun in her black flowing habit standing at the front of the

class, drawing the outline of a milk bottle on the blackboard. She whirled around, her veils and skirts and the long wooden rosary hanging from her waist swirling, and faced us, her seven-year-old charges. "This is the soul!" she proclaimed. Then, turning the chalk on its side, she filled in the outline with white and, pointing triumphantly at the bottle, announced, "This is the soul in the State of Grace!" Then, with her fingers she rubbed out several small circles inside the bottle. A corroded soul, weakened. "This is the soul when you have sinned venial sins!" Venial sins were small-fry: lying, stealing, being mean to your brother. You were still in the State of Grace, only not so much. Then she erased the white chalk until the bottle was empty. "This is the soul when you have sinned mortal sins. There is no grace in this soul! If this person died, this soul would go to hell!" Mortal sins were big ones: murder, adultery, worshiping false gods, not going to church on Sunday. Mortal sins equaled being out of the State of Grace and there was hell to pay. As Catholics we were lucky. We could trot off to confession, tell all, say our penance, and we'd have a full milk bottle again. It made terrifying sense to a seven-year-old.

But adult life isn't that simple. Perhaps the bigger the life, the bigger the potential for arrogance, for blindness, for wretchedness, for sinning and being sinned against. Jerry learned about these things the hard way, through his miserable experiences with drugs, his entrapment in a net of false assumptions, the claustrophobic quality of his enormous fame, and his curious work—standing up in front of 80,000 people and playing his soul out. What a life he had, both heroic and hubris-filled! Yet I feel that Jerry redeemed himself by transforming his suffering into art, and committing to love. "There are benefits to maturity," he mused one day. Allowing grace its place in our lives was one of them. I think he died in the State of Grace. I hope he's in heaven, because he was by nature a good and generous man, hard-working and thoughtful. His natural state was one of grace.

—Deborah Koons Garcia

2002

Amazing grace, how sweet the sound,

That saved a wretch like me,

but now am found,

I once was lost,

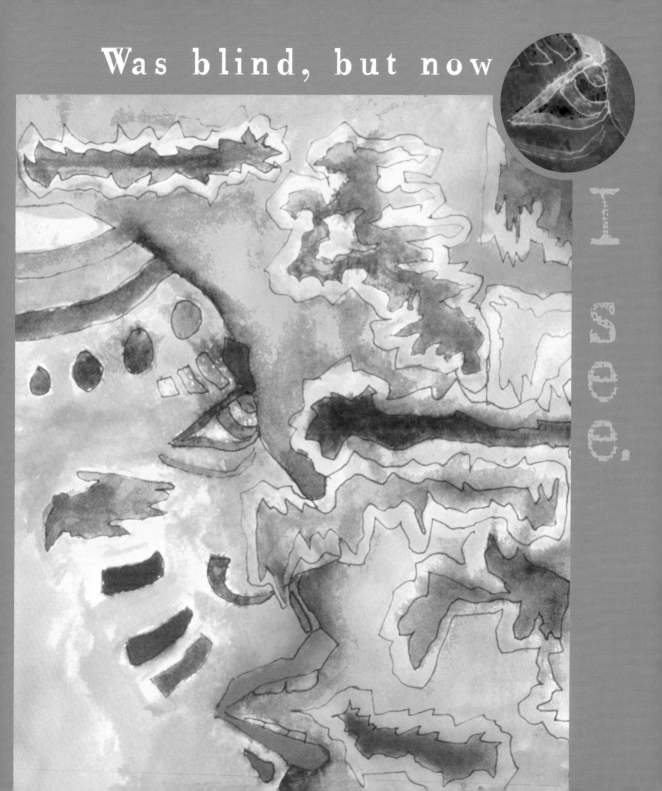

Was blind, but now I see.

'Twas grace that taught my heart to fear,

And grace my fears

relieved.

How precious
did that grace
appear,

The hour I first
believed!

When we've been there
ten thousand years

Bright shining as the sun,

to sing God's praise

We've no less days

Than when we first begun.

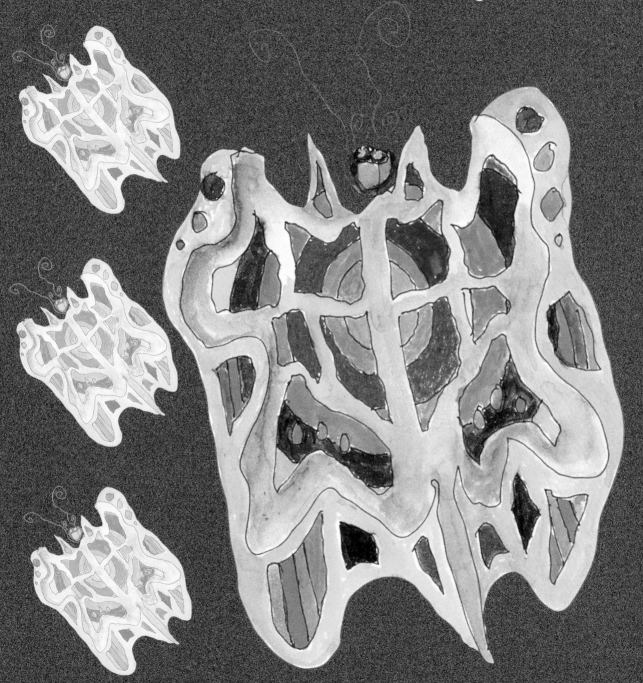

That saved

a wretch

like me.

I once was lost,

but now am found,

Was blind, but now

I see.

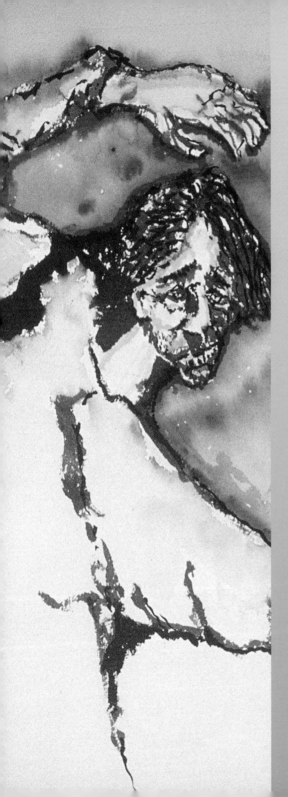

Jerry's Art

Untitled I,
1995

Demon

Trees, 1995

Snail Garden,
1995

Untitled I,
1995

Who Goes
There?

Another
Butterfly

Boy and Rabbit

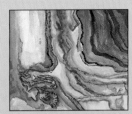

Liquid Torso

Unfinished Manuscript

Untitled 3

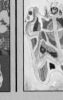

Another Butterfly

Liquid Torso

Unfinished Manuscript

Snail Garden, 1995

Paris in the Rain, 1991

Smoke Signals, 1990

Shaman, 1990

Demon, circa 1995

Chinese Dragon

Tropic

California Mission

Tree

Facets I, 1990

Untitled

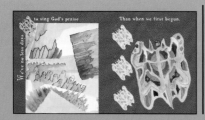

Greek Theatre Feet

Another
Butterfly

Red Meadow

Bag Lady

Who Goes There?

Bandito/South of the Border

Scales

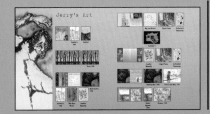

Fencing Class